THE DRAGONSITTER'S
Castle

THE DRAGONSITTER'S Castle

Josh Lacey

Illustrated by Garry Parsons

LITTLE, BROWN AND COMPANY
New York • Boston

Text copyright © 2013 by Josh Lacey
Illustrations copyright © 2013 by Garry Parsons
Text in excerpt from *The Dragonsitter's Island* copyright © 2014 by Josh Lacey
Illustrations in excerpt from *The Dragonsitter's Island* copyright © 2014
by Garry Parsons

Little, Brown and Company

Hachette Book Group
1290 Avenue of the Americas, New York, NY 10104
Visit us at lb-kids.com

Little, Brown and Company is a division of Hachette Book Group, Inc.
The Little, Brown name and logo are trademarks of Hachette Book Group, Inc.

The publisher is not responsible for websites (or their content) that are not owned
by the publisher.

First U.S. Edition: April 2016
Originally published in Great Britain in 2013 by Andersen Press Limited

Library of Congress Control Number: 2015945927

ISBN 978-0-316-38240-3

10 9 8 7 6 5 4 3 2 1

RRD-C

Printed in the United States of America

THE DRAGONSITTER'S Castle

Dear Uncle Morton,

I just tried calling you, but the phone made a funny noise. Have you changed your number?

I wanted to tell you your dragons are here.

They must have arrived in the middle of the night. When I came down for breakfast, Ziggy was sitting on the patio, peering through the window, looking very sorry for herself.

I didn't even see baby Arthur. I thought Ziggy had left him at home. Then I realized he was tucked under her tummy, trying to keep warm.

They're feeling better now that we've given them some toast and let them sit by the heater.

Have they come to say merry Christmas? Are
you coming, too? I'm afraid we didn't get you a
present, but there's lots of turkey left and about
a million brussels sprouts.

Love,

Eddie

Dear Uncle Morton,

Your dragons are still here. They have eaten the entire contents of the fridge and most of the cans in the cupboard, too.

Arthur also swallowed three spoons and the remote control.

Mom says they will probably come out the other end, but I'm not really looking forward to that.

She wants to know when you are coming to collect the dragons.

We're leaving first thing on Thursday morning, so she asks if you could you get here by Wednesday afternoon at the latest.

Eddie

Dear Uncle Morton,

Your phone is still making the same noise. Mom says you've probably been cut off because you haven't paid your bill.

Does that mean you didn't get my e-mails, either?

So, what are we supposed to do with the dragons?

We're leaving first thing tomorrow morning.

Mom has to catch the 9:03, or she won't arrive in time for the meet and greet with Swami Ticklemore.

She is going on that yoga retreat like you suggested. She says she deserves it after the year she's had.

I asked if the dragons could stay here without us, but she said, "No way, José," which you have to admit is fair enough after last time.

Emily and I are going to stay with Dad in his new house. He says it's a castle, but Dad's always saying things like that.

I called him and asked if we could bring the dragons.

He said no, because his new girlfriend, Bronwen, is allergic to fur.

I told him dragons don't have fur, but he said even so.

So please come and get them ASAP.

Eddie

P.S. I've been waiting with my rubber gloves, but there's still no sign of those spoons or the remote control.

Dear Uncle Morton,

Mom says if you're not here in the next ten minutes, she'll leave the dragons in the street and they can take care of themselves.

I said you couldn't possibly get from Scotland to here in ten minutes, and she said worse things happen at sea.

I have literally no idea what she meant.

Now she and Dad are shouting at each other just like they used to when they were still married.

If you get this in the next ten minutes, please call us!

Eddie

Dear Uncle Morton,

I hope you haven't left already to pick up the dragons, because they're not at our house anymore.

Dad said they could come to his castle after all.

I don't know what changed his mind, but he did say the Welsh have always had a soft spot for dragons.

Luckily, Bronwen had stayed behind, so there was room for all five of us in the car.

Dad was worried about his seats, but I told him dragons can be very careful with their claws if they want to, and I'm glad to say they were.

7

We got a lot of strange looks on the highway, and there was a nasty moment when Arthur flapped his wings and almost got sucked out the window. But now we've arrived at Dad's new castle, and we're all fine.

It really is a castle!

There's a moat and half a drawbridge and a rusty old cannon by the front door.

Dad bought it cheap because the previous owner had lost all his money.

He is going to convert it into apartments and sell them off and finally make his millions.

Our bedroom is in a turret. There's a little wooden staircase which goes to the top and you can see for miles.

The only problem is it's freezing. Dad says that's the price you have to pay for living in a historical building, but I don't see why he couldn't just buy some heaters.

Here is the address:

Manawydan Castle
Llefelys
Near Llandrindod Wells
Powys, Wales
UNITED KINGDOM

Dad says please come and pick up the dragons ASAP because he and Bronwen are having a party on New Year's Eve, and they want everything to go perfectly.

Eddie

Dear Uncle Morton,

I forgot to say: Please bring some medicine for Ziggy.

She's got a terrible cold.

When she sneezes, little jets of fire come out of her nostrils. I hope it's not contagious.

Eddie

Hi Eddie,

I'm very sorry that I haven't replied before, but my communication with the outside world has been severed for more than a week by the thick layer of snow smothering my island. I even had to dig a path from my back door to the shed so I could bring back some dry logs for the fire.

My boat was frozen solid, so I couldn't possibly get to the mainland, and I spent the festive season alone, reading several excellent books and eating my way through whatever I could find at the back of my cupboard. Luckily, I had stocked up on my last trip to France, so I spent

a very happy Christmas eating duck paté and drinking some wonderful eggnog.

The dragons weren't so content. They huddled by the fire for the first couple of days, then disappeared. How very sensible of them to come and find you.

I polished off the last of my food last night and raised a red flag. Luckily, Mr. McDougall saw it

first thing this morning and came to rescue me in his boat.

I'm now checking my e-mails in his house. He sends season's greetings, by the way, and hopes to meet you soon.

I'm sorry to hear that Ziggy is unwell. Please try to keep her and Arthur comfortable until I arrive. I wouldn't want them to fly any farther south. They'd only get lost.

Mr. McDougall's nephew Gordon is giving me a lift to the train station. I have just checked the schedule. If I make my connections at Glasgow and Crewe, I should be with you tonight.

With lots of love from your affectionate uncle,

Morton

Dear Uncle Morton,

We're all very glad you're coming!

We're going out now to pick up the drinks for the party, but we'll be back by six o'clock.

If you get here early, Dad says the pub in the village is excellent, although he advises against the pickled eggs.

Bronwen says please don't bring any more snow, because we've got enough already. It came down last night, and we're now knee-deep in it.

We just went out to make a snowman, but we made something much better instead. Here's a picture. Can you guess what it is?

16

Arthur jumped around all over the place, making funny little barking noises, then challenged the snowdragon to a duel.

He melted a hole in its middle, which made him even more confused.

If the snow hasn't melted by the morning, will you help us make another?

Eddie

From: Edward Smith-Pickle

To: Morton Pickle

Date: Friday, December 30

Subject: Medicine

📎 **Attachments:** Hot water bottle

Dear Uncle Morton,

I'm really sorry. Arthur has caught his mom's cold.

It's my fault. I shouldn't have let him play in the snow.

I've given them hot water bottles, but they won't stop sneezing.

I hope you're bringing lots of medicine.

Eddie

Dear Uncle Morton,

We're going to bed now, but Dad will leave the door unlocked. We've made up a bed for you on the sofa in the sitting room, which is actually the warmest room in the castle.

I asked if you could stay for the party, but Dad said only without the dragons, so I suppose that means no.

I wish you could. It really is going to be a great party.

We've been helping Bronwen make the appetizers. There's smoked salmon and mini pizzas and cheese cubes and chicken wings, plus enough chips to fill twelve huge bowls.

Bronwen wants us to take everyone's coats when they arrive. Dad bought about a million fireworks to set off at midnight.

Dad said we can stay up to watch. I reminded him that Emily is only five, but he said it would be good for her.

I said Mom would be furious, and he said she'd be furious with whatever he did, which is probably true.

Eddie

Dear Uncle Morton,

Are you stuck in a snowdrift?

I hope not, because Dad is going to evict the dragons if you're not here by lunchtime.

I said he can't make sick dragons sleep outside in this weather, and he said tough luck.

Eddie

Sorry about delay. Helping McD rescue sheep
from unexpected avalanche.

Gordon taking me to station now. Will be with
you by 4:00 p.m. at the latest.

M

From: Edward Smith-Pickle

To: Morton Pickle

Date: Saturday, December 31

Subject: Appetizers

📎 **Attachments:** Crime scene

Dear Uncle Morton,

Could you try to get here before 4:00 p.m.? The dragons have ruined the party, so we have to leave the castle right now.

It happened when we came back from making the second snowdragon. I was just taking off my boots when I heard a terrible scream. I thought Emily must have seen another mouse. I ran into the kitchen and found a scene of total devastation.

There were puff pastries everywhere. The floor was covered with chips. Somehow twenty deviled eggs had gotten stuck to the ceiling. The entire platter of smoked salmon was gone, including all six lemons and the pepper grinder.

Bronwen said she'd only stepped outside for a second to get another jar of mayonnaise, but she must have been gone for longer than that. Not even Ziggy can eat 600 appetizers in one second.

I thought the dragons might at least look guilty, but I've never seen anyone looking so pleased with themselves.

The good thing is they must be getting better if they're hungry.

I didn't say that to Dad, because I could see he wasn't in the mood.

When Bronwen finally stopped shouting, she said in a quiet voice that enough was enough and it was them or her.

Dad said he was sorry, but he hardly knew the dragons and that they were big enough to look after themselves. And then he said some things about you, Uncle Morton, which you probably don't want to know.

I said if the dragons left then I was leaving, too.

Emily said so was she.

Dad told us not to be ridiculous, but we weren't.

You'll find us at the castle gates.

I hope you'll be here soon, Uncle Morton, because the forecast is for more snow.

Eddie

From: Edward Smith–Pickle

To: Morton Pickle

Date: Saturday, December 31

Subject: Back again

Dear Uncle Morton,

You'll be glad to hear we're back in the castle. It's not much warmer than outside, but at least we won't get covered in snow.

Dad came to get us. He made a deal with Bronwen. She doesn't mind the dragons staying if they're locked in our turret at the top of the castle. We have to stay with them till you arrive.

See you at 4:00 p.m., if not before.

Eddie

From: Edward Smith-Pickle

To: Morton Pickle

Date: Saturday, December 31

Subject: 4:00 p.m. at latest?????

Attachments: The first guests

Dear Uncle Morton,

It's 8:20 and the first guests have just arrived.

We're still stuck in the turret with your dragons.

I said what about the coats, and Bronwen said the coats could take care of themselves.

Where are you?

E

Hi Eddie,

I'm sure you're safely tucked into bed at this unearthly hour of the morning, but I wanted to wish you a very happy New Year.

I'm terribly sorry that I haven't reached you yet, but the avalanche turned out to be more serious than first thought, and I've been helping Mr. McDougall retrieve a hundred and eleven sheep that had been scattered around the hills.

They are all now safely in his barn. We just celebrated midnight with a chorus of "Auld Lang Syne" and a bottle that the McDougalls had been saving for a special occasion.

Gordon will give me a lift to the station first thing. I should be with you in time for dinner.

Morton

Dear Uncle Morton,

I'm very glad to hear you're finally coming to Wales, but please don't go to the castle. We're not there anymore. We are staying at the Manawydan Arms in Llefelys.

You're probably wondering why we're not staying at the castle, and the reason is very simple. Ziggy burned it down.

You can't exactly blame her (although Dad does) because she didn't mean to.

It happened last night. The four of us were in the turret, looking out the window, watching cars pulling up and guests hurrying into the castle.

I now know you were four hundred miles away, Uncle M, but I didn't at the time and I kept hoping to see you.

Emily and I had our blankets, but the dragons were freezing. There was snow coming through the holes in the windows. I was worried the two poor shivering dragons would get pneumonia.

Then I had a great idea. Our room had a fireplace. Why not use it?

I sneaked downstairs and grabbed some wood and a newspaper. Dad had taught me how to scrunch up the paper and make a pyramid from the kindling. He did tell me to never light a fire without adult supervision, but we were so cold I had to do something. I was just looking around for some matches when Ziggy sneezed and the whole pile burst into flames.

For a moment, we were lovely and warm.

Then a rocket whooshed past my left ear and exploded against the ceiling.

Someone must have left a box of fireworks in the kindling basket. Maybe I picked some fireworks up by mistake when I was gathering wood. They do look very much like ordinary sticks.

Another rocket shot across the room and through the window, smashing the one pane of glass that wasn't already broken.

A pinwheel spun across the floor and down the stairs.

One of the fireworks must have set fire to a curtain or a blanket because suddenly the turret was in flames.

Emily screamed so loudly I thought my eardrums might burst. I was trying to stay calm, but I was

beginning to panic, too. It was extremely hot and quite difficult to breathe, and our route downstairs was blocked by a thick wall of black smoke.

There was only one way out.

We had to go up.

Emily and I charged to the top of the turret, followed by the dragons. Fireworks were exploding in every direction. Down on the ground, I could see guests flooding out of the castle.

We screamed for help, but no one could hear us.

Luckily, Ziggy knew what to do. She bent her neck and flapped her wings.

All three of us hopped aboard.

When we took off, there was a huge cheer from all of Dad's guests. They must have thought we were part of the display.

I had expected Ziggy to land beside Dad, but she flew into the woods and landed under a big tree.

Once she was on the ground, she refused to move. She and Arthur just curled up in the snow. I said it wasn't a sensible place for a nap if you've got a cold, but they didn't care.

Emily and I had to walk home. We were both shivering. Emily's lips turned blue.

Just when I thought we might die of frostbite, I

heard someone shouting our names. I shouted back. It was Dad. He came running through the trees and gathered us both up in his arms and said he'd thought we were dead. I'd never seen him cry before.

The fire had died down by the time we got back to the castle. Dad gave the firefighters a crate of champagne to say thank you. The labels had burned off the bottles, but they didn't mind.

Emily and I are sharing a room at the Manawydan Arms. Dad is asleep next door. He's probably going to kill me when he wakes up.

I wish I could say happy New Year, but it really isn't.

Eddie

Dear Uncle Morton,

I don't know where you are or what's happened to you, but if you do ever get here, we are still staying at the Manawydan Arms. It's the only pub in the village, and Dad says you can't miss it.

The three of us went back to the castle today. There's not much left, just a few blackened walls and some smoldering timbers.

In case you're wondering why there are only three of us, Bronwen has gone to her mother's in Aberystwyth. She and Dad had a big fight last night.

Bronwen said sorry to me and Emily for her

language, but I said she shouldn't worry, we'd heard it all before when Mom and Dad were getting divorced, and worse, too.

Bronwen said Dad obviously hadn't learned from his mistakes, and he said she was right about that. That was when she left.

There's still no sign of the dragons. Dad says they're old enough to look after themselves, but Arthur certainly isn't. And I'm not sure if Ziggy is, either, especially when she's got a cold.

Also, Dad says I owe him a new castle.

I thought he was joking, but he's not.

Apparently, he borrowed all the money to buy the castle, and now he'll never be able to pay it back.

He's ruined, and it's my fault.

Today is only the second of January, but this is already turning out to be the worst year of my life.

Eddie

From: Edward Smith-Pickle

To: Morton Pickle

Date: Tuesday, January 3

Subject: Lost

Dear Uncle Morton,

I'm a terrible dragonsitter. There's still no sign of Ziggy or Arthur, and I have no idea where they might be.

There's no sign of Bronwen, either, but Dad said not to worry about her, because there are a lot more fish in the sea.

Emily said he could get married to Mom again, but Dad said he'd been married to her once already and that was enough for any man.

Dad is going back to the castle today. Emily and I are going with him, and we'll search the forest for your dragons.

Eddie

From: Morton Pickle

To: Edward Smith-Pickle

Date: Wednesday, January 4

Subject: Re: Lost

Attachments: Lower Bisket church

Dear Eddie,

I'm terribly sorry to hear about the castle. Please pass on my apologies to your father. I don't have the funds to pay for a new castle, but I will help in any way that I can.

I'm sorry that I haven't reached you yet, but there has been a crisis in the village. The weight of all the snow on the church roof caused it to collapse. Mr. McDougall and I, along with all other able-bodied men and women, were called upon to help.

You will be glad to hear we have repaired the worst of the damage. I'm going to the station now and shall be with you this afternoon.

Don't worry about Ziggy and Arthur. I have read
that the caves of North Wales were once full
of dragons, so they have probably sniffed out
some distant relatives. We shall search for them
together when I arrive.

Morton

Dear Uncle Morton,

We have reserved a room for you at the Manawydan Arms.

It's Trivia Night tonight and there's a cash prize, which would be really useful now that I'm saving up to buy a new castle.

If you get here in time, you could join our team. I bet you're brilliant at trivia games.

We spent today at the castle again, but there's still no sign of your dragons. I hope you're right about them hiding in a cave. I'm just worried they won't be warm enough.

Eddie

From: Morton Pickle

To: Edward Smith-Pickle

Date: Thursday, January 5

Subject: Re: Trivia Night

Delayed again. Leaving now.

Sorry to miss trivia.

M

Dear Uncle Morton,

The Manawydan Arms is full. They won't reserve a room for you because you didn't use the one they kept for you yesterday, but you can sleep on the floor in ours.

Dad is driving us home first thing tomorrow morning, so you can keep the room if you want to stay here while you search for the dragons.

Don't worry about missing Trivia Night. We came in second and won a prize!

When I told Dad I would add the cash to his savings for a new castle, he told me not to be ridiculous and bought a round of drinks for everyone in the pub.

I suppose that's what Mom means about him being useless with money.

He got a piece of good news yesterday, so there was something to celebrate. The man from the insurance company thinks his policy should pay out in full because the fire was caused by misadventure and/or faulty equipment.

Emily told him that the fire was actually caused by a dragon trying to keep warm.

The insurance man said he'd never heard that one before.

Dad gave me a look, so I kept quiet, and we pretended that Emily has a vivid imagination.

See you later.

Eddie

From: Morton Pickle

To: Edward Smith-Pickle

Date: Friday, January 6

Subject: Re: Our last night

📎 **Attachments:** Home sweet home

Dear Eddie,

I hope you're safely home by now. I'm terribly sorry that I never reached Wales and didn't get a chance to see your father's castle. However, it all turns out to have been for the best.

I was finally ready to catch a train yesterday when I remembered that you had asked me to bring some medicine. I have a large stock in my bathroom cabinet, so I borrowed Mr. McDougall's boat and whizzed across the channel to my island.

I moored the boat, hurried up the path to the house, and was just reaching for my keys when who should I see lounging on the lawn....

There they were, my two dragons, enjoying this morning's unexpected sunshine. They showed no shame for causing so much trouble. All they wanted was a snack and a belly rub, and I happily was able to provide both.

You'll be glad to hear that their coughs and colds are entirely cured. I'm sorry they didn't behave themselves, but thanks again for looking after them so well.

Perhaps this year you will finally come and visit us?

Love,

Morton, Ziggy, and Arthur

From: Edward Smith–Pickle

To: Morton Pickle

Date: Saturday, January 7

Subject: Home

📎 **Attachments:** Yoga

Dear Uncle Morton,

I'm very pleased the dragons are safe. I was getting quite worried they might never be found.

We're home, too, and everything is fine.

Mom says THANK YOU for recommending the yoga retreat. (She asked me to put that in capital

letters.) She says she's never felt so relaxed in her entire life.

It's true. She didn't even mind about the burn marks on our pajamas.

She wants to go back ASAP, so maybe I could come and stay then?

Happy New Year!

And lots of love from your favorite nephew,

Eddie

P.S. Will you keep looking in Arthur's poop? Mom says the spoons don't matter, but it would be nice if we could turn on the TV.

What's next for Eddie & Ziggy?

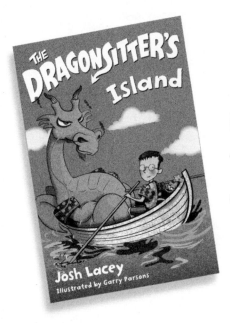

Don't miss their fourth adventure!

Turn the page for a sneak peek.

COMING SOON

Dear Uncle Morton,

Where is the key to your house?

We arrived on your island this morning, but we couldn't get in.

Mom thought you might have left it under a stone or buried in a flowerpot, so we searched everywhere.

Emily discovered a silver necklace and I found two coins, but there was no sign of the key.

Through the window I could see your dragons going crazy. I don't know if they were happy to see us or just hungry, but Arthur was charging around and around the house, knocking over your furniture, and Ziggy wouldn't stop breathing fire.

Luckily, Mr. McDougall was still here. He was sure you wouldn't mind if he broke a window.

Unfortunately, he couldn't open the front door from the inside, so we had to push the suitcases through the window and climb in after them.

Ziggy and Arthur are much happier now that we've given them our presents (a big box of malted milk balls for her and three packs of mini chocolate eggs for him).

They also ate our leftover sandwiches from the train and the book I was reading. Luckily, the book wasn't very good.

Emily and I are going to search your house for the key. Mom says if we can't find it, we'll have to go home tomorrow and the dragons can fend for themselves.

I said I wouldn't mind climbing in and out of the window for the whole week, but Mom told me not to be ridiculous.

Have you taken it by mistake? Didn't you leave a spare anywhere?

Love from your favorite nephew,

Eddie

Dear Uncle Morton,

We haven't found the key, but I have found your phone. Mom called you to leave another message and I heard it ringing behind the sofa.

I hope you don't need it in Outer Mongolia. I put it on the mantelpiece with the necklace and the coins.

Mr. McDougall has gone back to the mainland in his boat. Emily says it's creepy being the only people here, but I like it.

Thanks for your instructions and the map. Emily and Mom took hours unpacking their bags, so I've been exploring. I climbed Dead Man's Cairn and walked all the way along the beach to Lookout Point.

Arthur sat on my shoulder like a parrot. At first I was worried he might burn my ear off, but he hasn't been breathing any fire at all. Isn't he old enough?

Eddie

From: Edward Smith–Pickle

To: Morton Pickle

Date: Saturday, February 18

Subject: Cans

📎 **Attachments:** Accidental number 2

Dear Uncle Morton,

We have now searched your house, your garden, and quite a lot of your island, but we still can't find the key. Please write back ASAP and tell us where it is.

Mom is dead serious about leaving tomorrow. It's not just because of the key. It's the poop, too.

Ziggy did one in the kitchen and another by the back door.

I know it's not her fault. She can't fit through the window, and she has to go somewhere. I just wish she could hold them in until we've found the key.

Also, Mom is asking where the can opener is.

We brought some food, but not enough because you told us your cupboard was full of provisions. Unfortunately, all the provisions are in cans.

I'm sure I could open them with a knife, but Mom won't let me because we'd need a helicopter to get to the nearest hospital.

Eddie

Dear Uncle Morton,

I'm very sorry, but we are leaving your island.

This morning, Mom found another piece of poop in the kitchen. She said that was the final straw.

I did suggest staying here on my own, but Mom said, "Not a chance, buster."

She has already raised the red flag. I just looked through the telescope and saw Mr. McDougall preparing his boat on the mainland. I suppose he'll be here in about fifteen minutes.

I have given all our spare food to the dragons. I have also put some cans on the floor in case they're better at opening them than me.

I will ask Mr. McDougall to come here every day and feed them until you get back.

Eddie

Dear Uncle Morton,

We're still here.

We never left. Mr. McDougall wouldn't let us.

He said the dragons can't stay on your island unsupervised.

Mom asked why not, and Mr. McDougall explained that one of his sheep went missing in the middle of the night. This morning, he found bloodstains on the grass and a trail of wool leading down to the water.

I don't know why he blames your dragons. Arthur can hardly fly and Ziggy can't even leave the house, so there is no way either of them could have gotten from here to the mainland, let alone murdered a sheep. But Mr. McDougall says they are the prime suspects.

Now he has gone home again, and we're stuck here without a key or any food.

Eddie

Dear Eddie,

I am so sorry to hear about your troubles with the front door. I was sure that I had discussed the key with your mother when we talked last week. Has she forgotten our conversation?

This is what I said to her: If you walk down to the end of the garden, you will discover a stone statue of a yellow–headed vulture perched in the shrubbery. The key is hidden under its left talon.

Please be very careful when you lift it up. That vulture has great sentimental value. It was given to me by the sculptor himself, who lives in a small hut beside the Amazon, and I carried it all the way back from Brazil wrapped in an old shirt.

I have been in touch with Mr. McDougall, who is understandably upset about the loss of his sheep. I assured him that the dragons couldn't be responsible. He didn't appear to be entirely convinced, but I'm sure he'll find the real culprit soon.

All is good here in Ulaanbaatar. I have discovered some fascinating and unexpected information at the National Library, so my visit has already been worthwhile.

The only problem is the weather. Walking the streets without a coat on would be certain death, and even the Reading Room is so cold that no one removes their hats or scarves.

Unfortunately, it's impossible to turn the pages of an old book while wearing gloves, so my fingers are like icicles by the end of the day. Every evening, after leaving the library, I warm myself up at a local restaurant with a bowl of yak stew and a glass of the local brew—a white drink called Airag, made from fermented horse milk. It tastes better than it sounds.

I'm very sorry about the can opener. Have you looked in the silverware drawer?

With love from your affectionate uncle,

Morton

Dear Uncle Morton,

We found the key!

And we were very careful with the statue.

Mom says you definitely didn't mention it last week. She would have remembered if you had.

You don't have to worry about the can opener. It wasn't in the silverware drawer or anywhere else, but Mr. McDougall's nephew Gordon jetted across this morning in his speedboat and delivered another. He also brought a box of crackers and some nice cheese.

After he had gone, I found Mom and Emily whispering in the kitchen.

When I asked what was going on, Emily said they were talking about Gordon. Mom thinks he's very handsome.

I don't know if he's handsome, but I like his boat. He said he'll take me for a ride around the island to see the puffins.

Love,

Eddie

Dear Uncle Morton,

Gordon has been here again. He took us to Lower Bisket in his speedboat to buy food and supplies.

Emily thinks it was a date.

Mom told her not to be ridiculous, but she did turn bright pink.

Apparently, Mr. McDougall is on a rampage. Another sheep went missing last night.

I asked Gordon to tell him that the dragons spent the whole night in my bedroom, with the door shut and the windows locked.

Gordon said I should do the same tonight because Mr. McDougall is planning to stay up from dusk until dawn with a thermos of hot tea and a rifle.

Otherwise everything is fine. We bought lots of food in the Lower Bisket General Store. The dragons are happy. Even Mom is in a good mood. We went for a walk on the beach this afternoon, and she said it's so peaceful and beautiful she can almost understand why you want to live here.

Eddie

From: Morton Pickle

To: Edward Smith-Pickle

Date: Tuesday, February 21

Subject: Re: More sheep

Dear Eddie,

I have to admit that I am worried by your last message. I know from personal experience that Mr. McDougall is an excellent shot.

On that particular occasion, he wasn't aiming at me, but I should not like to find myself in his sights.

Please make sure that you keep the dragons under observation at all times. I cannot believe that they could be responsible for attacking his livestock, but I wouldn't want to expose them to any unnecessary risks.

I hope your mother enjoyed her date with Gordon. Isn't he a little young for her?

Morton

THE DRAGONSITTER Series

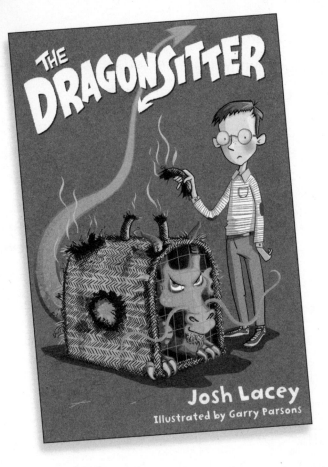

THE DRAGONSITTER

Josh Lacey

Illustrated by Garry Parsons

THE DRAGONSITTER Takes Off

Josh Lacey
Illustrated by Garry Parsons

THE DRAGONSITTER'S Castle

Josh Lacey
Illustrated by Garry Parsons

THE DRAGONSITTER'S Island

Josh Lacey
Illustrated by Garry Parsons

Coming in Fall 2016

COLLECT
THEM
ALL!

If you enjoyed **THE DRAGONSITTER'S Castle**, you might also like these series, available now!

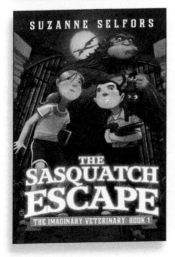

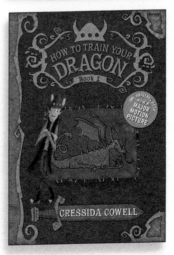

Don't miss a single **SPACE TAXI** adventure!

BOOK 1

BOOK 2

BOOK 3

BOOK 4

Meet

LOLA LEVINE

Join spunky second-grader Lola on all her escapades. She's sure to warm your heart!

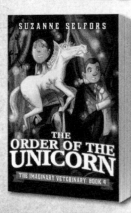
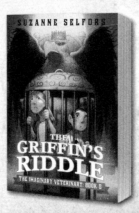

About the Author

JOSH LACEY is the author of many books for children, including *The Island of Thieves*, *Bearkeeper*, and the Grk series. He worked as a journalist, a teacher, and a screenwriter before writing his first book, *A Dog Called Grk*. Josh lives in London with his wife and daughters.

About the Illustrator

GARRY PARSONS has illustrated several books for children and is the author and illustrator of *Krong!*, winner of the Perth and Kinross Picture Book Award. Garry lives in London.